A MESSAGE TO PARENTS

It is of vital importance for parents to read good books to young children in order to aid the child's psychological and intellectual development. At the same time as stimulating the child's imagination and awareness of his environment, it creates a positive relationship between parent and child. The child will gradually increase his basic vocabulary and will soon be able to read books alone.

Brown Watson has published this series of books with these aims in mind. By collecting this inexpensive library, parent and child are provided with hours of pleasurable and profitable reading.

THE CHRISTMAS ELF

Text by Maureen Spurgeon
Illustrated by Mimi Everett

Brown Watson
ENGLAND

Everyone in Santa Claus' little workshop had to agree – Eddie the elf was really a very nice person. He was always smiling and cheerful – never cross or grumpy. And he was always ready to help.

"I'll carry that!" he cried when he saw Dame Jolly bringing in the teacups. "Give your arms a rest."

Poor Eddie! He didn't mean to make Dame Jolly spill the tea! "Oh, Eddie . . ." she sighed. "Don't worry!" grinned Eddie — something he often said when things went wrong. "I'll soon wipe it up."

"Oh dear, no!" groaned Fixit the handyman. "Not with my brand new sack!"

"Sorry!" grinned Eddie – something else he often said. "I'll wash it."

"No, wait!" cried Fixit. "There are some toy cars inside!"

SMASH! Eddie thought it was a good idea to tip the cars out on to the floor!

CRASH! Down fell Pink the Pixie and Maid Merry!

"Sorry . . ." said Eddie, again.

"That's what you always say," groaned Fixit. "Did you remember to take over that box of spinning tops Santa Claus wanted?"
"Sorry!" gasped Eddie. "I forgot."

Just then, Santa Claus came in.
He did not look very pleased.
"All the paintboxes have been
mixed up with the skittles!" he
said. "Who packed this sack?"
"Sorry . . ." said Eddie.

"Humph! You can't carry on like this, Eddie," grunted Santa Claus, looking around at the mess.
"Sorry," said poor Eddie.
"I really do mean to help".

"I know, I know," said Santa Claus.
"Try and help Tolly, the Teddy Bear
maker, will you?" Eddie just
nodded in reply. He knew he had
to show that he could work well.
And Tolly did need help.

"Er, just start tidying up for now," said Tolly, when Eddie asked what he could do to help.
"I've got to try and get so many Teddy Bears finished and packed up before Christmas Eve."

Kind-hearted Eddie did feel sorry for him. Suppose, he thought, just suppose he made some Teddy Bears for Tolly. Santa Claus would know what a good helper he was, then!

He was soon busy, cutting and
stitching, snipping and sewing.
The seams were a bit crooked
and one ear looked bigger than
the other. But, Eddie was very
pleased with his work!

"Only the thread to cut, now," he thought. Instead, he cut a big hole in one paw! But he soon cut a patch of material to stick on top. He had just finished when Tolly gave a shout.

"Where's that piece of sparkly fur I left here? That's all I had!"
"Oh, don't worry about that," said Eddie. "See what I've made."
"Th-that patch!" choked Tolly. "It's cut it from my special fur!"

"Sorry . . ." said Eddie.
"Sorry?" cried Tolly. "I've got to finish off a batch of Teddy Bears!"
Santa Claus came in to see what all the shouting was about, his face grim and unsmiling.

"I'm going to a big shop in town,
tomorrow," he said at last. "You
can come with me, Eddie. And if
you can find any child who really
wants that Teddy Bear, I'll let you
stay in my workshop."

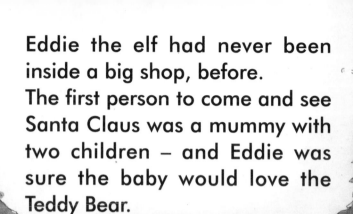

Eddie the elf had never been inside a big shop, before.
The first person to come and see Santa Claus was a mummy with two children – and Eddie was sure the baby would love the Teddy Bear.

But each time he tried to give it to the baby, he kept throwing it on the floor! In the end, it got so dusty and dirty that Eddie decided to try putting it in a Christmas stocking he saw hanging on the wall.

"Here!" cried one of the shop
assistants. "Who's put this old
thing in our Christmas display?
I'll put it out with the rubbish."
"No, wait!" shouted Eddie the elf.
"You can't do that!"

Santa Claus frowned across at Eddie. All the noise had upset a little girl and made her cry. The only thing Eddie could do now was search through the rubbish and just hope he would find the Teddy Bear . . .

And what a state the Teddy Bear was in! Dirty patches on his fur, stitches coming undone, bits of stuffing oozing out . . . who would want it, now? Eddie picked it up and went outside . . .

"Bear!" cried a little voice and a
hand reached out. "Nice bear!
Look, Mummy! Like Patchy!"
"No, darling," said the little girl's
mummy. "It doesn't belong to
you!"

"I'm sorry," the lady went on. "You see, Janey left her old rag doll on the bus last week, and it's made her so unhappy. She didn't even want the lovely, new doll Santa Claus tried to give her!"

"I thought I was the one who had made her cry," said Eddie. Janey's mummy just laughed.
"No!" she said. "You've made her smile." And Janey actually gave the Teddy Bear a big kiss!

Eddie smiled for the first time that day. And, when he said Janey could keep the bear she wanted so much, she and her mummy could not stop smiling. "Merry Christmas!" cried Eddie.